KU-602-831

DISNEY'S

Jungle Book

FLEETWAY BOOKS

Bagheera, the black panther, could hear anything. She knew all the jungle noises. Now, one evening, when she was out hunting for her dinner, a strange cry made her prick up her ears.

"That's not a bird," she said to herself. "Nor is it a baby wolf. It might be a monkey, though." She went forward carefully and there, by the river bank, she saw an old, half-sunken boat. There was a basket in the boat and inside the basket was a tiny boy. He was thin and dirty, and his frail little body shook with his sobbing.

Bagheera was a kindly creature. She knew all about
the dangers of the jungle. If she left the baby boy
there, she knew the crocodiles would come and eat him.
"I think I'll take you to Akela," she said to herself. She
picked up the basket in her mouth and set off with it.
From that moment the baby boy stopped crying and
fell asleep.

Akela was the biggest wolf in the jungle. With his
wife, Mother Wolf, he looked after their ten cubs,
as baby wolves are called. As soon as he saw the
baby boy that Bagheera had brought him he said,
"We'll take care of him. I'll call him Mowgli, and
he will be my son."

And so Mowgli grew up in the jungle. His brothers were the young wolves and they had lots of friends. Everyone was so kind to him that he would have been quite amazed if he had known that he had any other parents apart from Akela and Mother Wolf.

When Mowgli was ten, Bagheera the panther came to wish him a happy birthday. But she also brought him some very bad news. She told him that Shere Khan, the man-eating tiger, had heard that Mowgli was living in the jungle and he had set out to hunt for the boy.

That was bad news indeed! All the wolves of the jungle were summoned to a meeting. "What should be done to save Mowgli from the tiger?" asked Akela.

"Excuse me for saying so in front of Mother Wolf," said Bagheera the panther. "But I think Mowgli should go away. You know what Shere Khan is like. If he finds Mowgli he will eat him in one mouthful."

When she heard this, Mother Wolf ran to the edge of the cliff, so that no one could see her crying.

Bagheera went on: "I will talk to Mowgli. He is ten years old now, and he must learn to live like humans live. I will take him through the jungle to the village where people live."

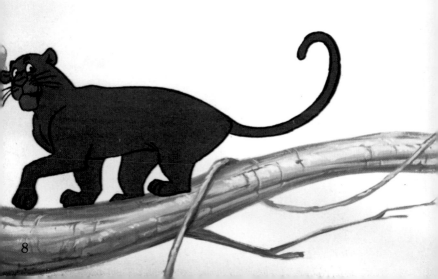

Everyone thought that
was a good idea. So next
day Mowgli said good-bye
to all his friends and
relatives. "I won't forget
any of you," he promised.
"When I'm a man I'll come
back to the jungle, and it
will be me who kills Shere
Khan!"

At the end of the first day's march through the jungle, though, little Mowgli was feeling far too tired to be brave. Bagheera decided that they would spend the night in a tree, and as soon as he had climbed on to a branch Mowgli fell fast asleep against his friend the panther.

11

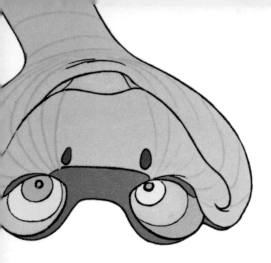

He was the first to wake up in the morning. "I think I'll just climb down and stretch my legs," he said to himself. As soon as he was on the ground he heard a hissing sound. He looked up and there was Kaa, the dreaded python. Already Kaa was hypnotising Mowgli with his wicked eyes and winding himself around the little boy.

In another second Kaa would have swallowed
Mowgli for breakfast. But at that moment
Bagheera the panther woke up. She gave a
mighty roar, struck out angrily at Kaa with her
sharp claws, and the python dropped Mowgli
and slithered away, hissing angrily.

"My goodness, you must be more careful!"
Bagheera scolded. Mowgli stared at his
feet, feeling a bit ashamed of himself. All
that day they marched through the jungle
again, and when night came they climbed
another tree to go to sleep.

Next day, a tremendous crashing noise in the
jungle woke him up early. He looked down from
the tree and there, coming through the jungle,
was a herd of marching elephants.

"Left, right! Left right!" shouted their leader.
And behind him the whole herd of elephants
marched in step with each other. "Wait for me!"
shouted Mowgli.

At the sound of Mowgli's shrill cry, the
elephants, who had never heard a human
voice before, all came to a stop together.
What a big bump that made!

Crash! Bang! Wallop!
"Someone has their big feet on my
trunk!" cried one elephant. "Who's that
climbing up my back?" shouted another.

"Be quiet at once, all of you!" ordered the elephant leader. "Everyone get back in line!" The elephants obeyed immediately. "And now," commanded the elephant leader, "let's have a big blast from everyone, just to give us all a lot of confidence." All the elephants raised their trunks to the sky and sounded a tremendous trumpeting noise.

"Now," said the elephant leader. "Which one of you cried out just now?" No one moved.

The elephants all looked very serious. All, that is, except the baby elephant at the end of the line, who laughed and laughed. Someone else was laughing, too. That was Mowgli, who had joined the baby elephant at the end of the line . . .

It was then that the elephant leader saw
Mowgli. "Who are you?" he roared. "I've
never seen an animal in shorts before!" He
picked up Mowgli in his trunk just as if he
were a feather. "Was it you who cried out?" he
roared.

"Stop, stop!"

The elephant leader recognised at once the voice of Bagheera the panther. "Put the boy down and I'll tell you all about him."

The elephant leader, who was a good friend of Bagheera, did as he was told, and then Bagheera said: "The boy's name is Mowgli and he is different from other human beings. He grew up with the wolves in the jungle and he's our friend. But now I'm taking him to where people live, because the tiger is after him."

Actually, Mowgli really wasn't afraid of Shere Khan
at all. He didn't want to go to these village people
that everyone kept talking about. He much preferred
to go and visit his funny friend Baloo.

Baloo was a lovely old bear. Although he was a bit too
old for some of Mowgli's games, as soon as Mowgli
jumped on his back he was quite happy to take him
for a ride.

Baloo was very good, too, at gathering delicious
jungle fruits. "It's time we had something nice to
eat," the old bear said.
"Good idea, Baloo," said Mowgli, rubbing his
tummy.
"We'll start with some honey," said Baloo. "And
then we'll have some juicy cactus berries. Oh, what
a fine feast we're going to have."

"After that," cried Mowgli, "we'll
finish off with some bananas!"
"Another good idea," said Baloo,
and he swung a banana tree branch
down so that Mowgli could reach it.

When they had finished
eating, Mowgli's tummy
began to feel very funny.
He had eaten too much.
Baloo, who loved to sing,
made up a song:
"If you've had too much
to eat,
Gently, gently raise your
feet.
Lift up each arm,
Keeping very calm,
As you smooth away
that nasty indigestion.
A little song, a little
dance,
A little stroll (but not a
prance)
Smooths away that
nasty indigestion!"

The two friends were making such a noise with their
song and dance that Bagheera came running to see
what was the matter. "Baloo!" she cried. "You ought to
be ashamed! You're making so much noise, Shere
Khan's bound to hear you!"

Baloo's answer was to burst out laughing. That
made Bagheera so angry that she ran up a tree and
got ready to jump on the bear. But Baloo simply
caught hold of the panther's tail. He knew that
when you hold a panther's tail one thing she can't
do is jump!

When Baloo finally let go,
Bagheera ran off crossly.
Then Baloo floated down
the river like a boat, with
Mowgli on top of him!

"Well, that's a funny ship!" said some monkeys as
they watched the two friends floating by beneath their
tree.

"I know who they are," said one of the monkeys. "The
boat is Baloo and the sailor is Mowgli."

"Let's have some fun with them," said another. And
that's what they did.

Very quietly, one of the monkeys swung out of the tree and covered Mowgli's mouth with his hand. Another grabbed the boy by his feet and – *presto!* he was whisked up into the tree without sleepy old Baloo even knowing anything about it.

The monkeys took Mowgli to their king, who lived in a ruined palace. He was a nice king, and gave Mowgli a piece of banana. But Mowgli wanted to get away.

Then a big monkey arrived to see the king. Is it a monkey – or is it Baloo disguised with a coconut shell and coconut tree leaves?

Yes, it's Baloo! Mowgli was about to run to his
friend, but Baloo winked and with a secret sign
showed Mowgli the way out of the palace.

While Mowgli slipped out through the door, Baloo-the-bear-disguised-as-a-monkey entertained the monkey king with a dance. "*Badado, badadum, badado, badadom, pom, pom,*" sang Baloo. He shook his big tummy so much in time to the song that suddenly his coconut disguise fell off.
All the monkeys ran forward. "It isn't a monkey!" they cried. "It's Baloo the bear!"

Baloo rushed out of the king's palace and rejoined
Mowgli. But the monkey king was quick, too, and he
grabbed one of Mowgli's hands. Poor Mowgli was in the
middle of a tug-o'-war. And then the old stone column
which the monkey king was holding on to began to
crumble and collapse. Who do you think arrived at that
moment to get poor Mowgli out of trouble? Why,
Bagheera the black panther, of course!

41

As soon as they were in a safe place, Bagheera
snapped at Baloo: "Don't you understand, you
silly old bear, that Mowgli is in danger in the
jungle?"

"But he's my little friend," said Baloo, looking
miserable.

"Then you take him to the village where the people
live," said Bagheera. "But on one condition – no
more stupid games. Understand?"

Baloo nodded. "I understand," he said.

Off went the two friends, with Mowgli trying to cheer up
that silly old bear.

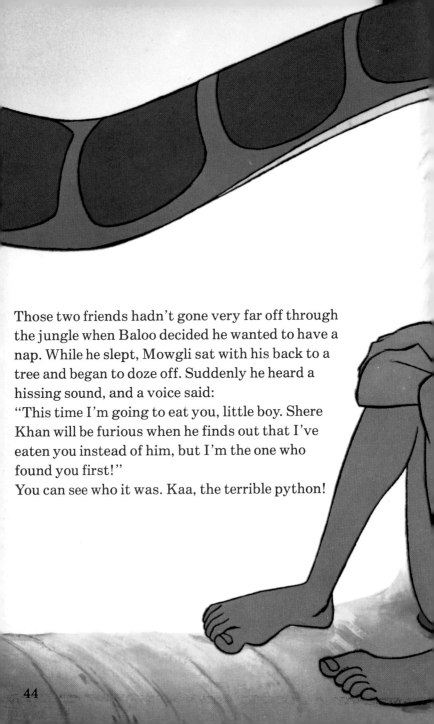

Those two friends hadn't gone very far off through the jungle when Baloo decided he wanted to have a nap. While he slept, Mowgli sat with his back to a tree and began to doze off. Suddenly he heard a hissing sound, and a voice said:

"This time I'm going to eat you, little boy. Shere Khan will be furious when he finds out that I've eaten you instead of him, but I'm the one who found you first!"

You can see who it was. Kaa, the terrible python!

"So you think you found him first, eh?" another voice thundered out close by.

Kaa drew back, dismayed. "Shere Khan!" he hissed. As the tiger hurled himself on the python, Mowgli jumped up and ran off as fast as he could.

"That was lucky!" he gasped. "It looks as if I've been saved by Shere Khan himself. Just wait until Bagheera hears that!"

47

Mowgli ran so fast that he soon reached the shores of the Black Lake. Mother Wolf had often told him about the Black Lake. "Keep away from it," she had always said. "It's full of white fish and poisonous spiders. And vultures who don't speak at all nicely live there."

Mowgli didn't see any spiders or any white fish. But there were plenty of vultures. They came running up to him.

"Hi, boyo, relax!" one said. "We're not going to eat you."

"We just want to kid you on," another one snickered. "What you doing, hangin' around these parts?" another said.

Well, thought Mowgli, it's true that they don't speak nicely, but they do seem quite friendly.

But while Mowgli was listening to the vultures' gossip, Shere Khan was creeping through the jungle grass on the shore of the Black Lake. When he saw Mowgli he lay quite still, waiting for the right moment to spring. "I enjoyed eating that python," he said to himself. "And now Mowgli will make a nice dessert."

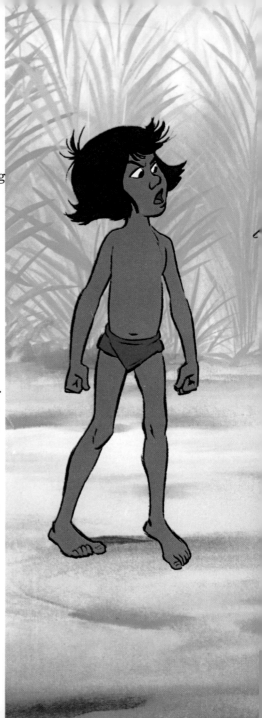

BOMP! The big tiger suddenly leapt out of the jungle and landed right in front of Mowgli. Fluttering and squawking, the vultures flew up into the sky.

"Say your prayers, boy!" roared Shere Khan. "I'm going to eat you!"

Mowgli shook with fear, but he tried not to show it. "You don't frighten me!" he said bravely. "Good, good!" roared Shere Khan. "In that case I won't have to run after you. I can just eat you here." And he opened his huge mouth to show his rows of sharp white teeth. "Oh, go away, you silly old striped blanket!" said Mowgli, who was trying very hard now not to show how frightened he was.

Silly old striped blanket! Shere Khan shook with rage. How dare Mowgli insult a fearsome tiger!

"Baloo!" cried Mowgli.

At that very moment the bear jumped from a tree and stood between Mowgli and the angry tiger. Baloo pulled a terribly frightening face – but was it really enough to scare off Shere Khan? Then both Baloo and Shere Khan suddenly stood still and sniffed. They could smell smoke!

Fire! Mowgli knew it was the one thing that really frightened Shere Khan. He lit a torch and set the jungle alight.

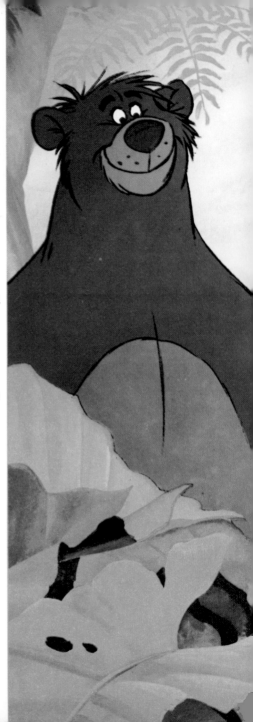

Then Mowgli ran and ran –
until he found his friend
Bagheera.

"We think it's better if
both Baloo and I take you
to the village where people
live," Bagheera said. So
they marched on through
the jungle for two more
days. Then Mowgli heard a
strange bird singing.

"Listen to that bird!" he
cried.

"Well, actually," said
Bagheera, "I don't think it
is a bird."

"It's a little girl, really,"
added the panther. "Her
parents are human beings,
just like your parents were."

Mowgli looked at Bagheera and Baloo, his wonderful
jungle friends, and a big lump came into his throat.
But then he looked at the little girl. She looked so
pretty as she filled her vase with water, and her
singing was beautiful.
"It is time for you to go and live with people now,"
Bagheera said gently. "Run to her, Mowgli."

"May I help you with your vase, miss?" asked Mowgli. The young girl nodded.

And so the little jungle boy went to live in the village where people live.

At the edge of the forest his two friends watched him go. They felt very sad. But they knew Mowlgi would be happy.